THE JUDGMENTAL FLOWER

BOYS TOWN Press

Boys Town, Nebraska

Written by Julia Cook   Illustrated by Anita DuFalla

The Judgmental Flower
Text and Illustrations Copyright © 2016 by Father Flanagan's Boys' Home
ISBN 978-1-944882-05-1

Published by the Boys Town Press
14100 Crawford St.
Boys Town, NE 68010

For a Boys Town Press catalog, call **1-800-282-6657**
or visit our website: **BoysTownPress.org**

Publisher's Cataloging-in-Publication Data

Names: Cook, Julia, 1964- author. | DuFalla, Anita, illustrator.

Title: The judgmental flower / written by Julia Cook ; illustrated by Anita DuFalla.

Description: Boys Town, NE : Boys Town Press, [2016] | Audience: Grades K-6. | Summary: When a Purple flower suddenly sprouts next to a Blue, all sorts of confusion ensues. Fortunately, Momma Blue is there to remind everyone about the beauty of diversity, including how the wind, rain, sun and bees treat all flowers the same regardless of the color of their petals or the size of their stems. Award-winning author Julia Cook shares a timely and valuable lesson about appreciating differences and embracing diversity in life and in friendships.--Publisher.

Identifiers: ISBN: 978-1-944882-05-1

Subjects: LCSH: Children--Life skills guides--Juvenile fiction. | Flowers--Juvenile fiction. | Plant diversity-- Juvenile fiction. | Prejudices--Juvenile fiction. | Difference (Psychology)--Juvenile fiction. | Individual differences--Juvenile fiction. | Equality--Juvenile fiction. | Friendship--Juvenile fiction. | Cultural pluralism--Juvenile fiction. | CYAC: Conduct of life--Fiction. | Flowers--Fiction. | Plants--Variation--Fiction. | Prejudices--Fiction. | Difference (Psychology)--Fiction. | Individuality --Fiction. | Equality--Fiction. | Friendship--Fiction. | Cultural pluralism--Fiction. | BISAC: JUVENILE FICTION / Social Themes / Prejudice & Racism. | JUVENILE FICTION / Social Themes / Friendship. | JUVENILE FICTION / Social Themes / Emotions & Feelings.

Classification: LCC: PZ7.C76984 J83 2016 | DDC: [E]--dc23

Printed in the United States
10 9 8 7 6 5 4 3 2

Boys Town Press is the publishing division of Boys Town, a national organization serving children and families.

I am a BLUE.

I live in a flower patch, in a yard, on a street, in a neighborhood, in a town, that's part of a city.

I have a GREAT BIG FAMILY and LOTS of friends. My roots run deep.

A few weeks ago, a purple started to grow by me.
I'd never seen a purple up close. He was so different.

I kept my DISTANCE.

"Purples don't belong here!" At least that's what the other blues say.

"This is supposed to be a blue flower patch."

"I don't like purple!" I told Mom.

"Why?"

"Because he's different."

"Well, there are lots of flowers in our patch who are different from you."

"I don't like them very much either. Some of them look kinda weird."

5

"And purple… he's not the same as me."

"I didn't know that everybody needed to be the same."

"Well, he's not blue… he's not like we are.
This is a blue flower patch, and he shouldn't be growing here."

"Who told you that?"

"Just about everyone I know."

"Well son, there are some flowers whose sole purpose in life is to show the rest of us how NOT to grow!"

"Does purple have roots like you?"

"I think so."

"Do his roots drink the same water as yours?"

"I guess."

7

"You can learn a lot from WATER.
It helps all flowers grow.
Big ones, tall ones, short ones, small ones…
It's FLOWER RESPECTFUL, you know."

8

"Does purple dance in the wind like you do?"

"He dances… but not like me."

"You can learn a lot from the **WIND**.
On every flower it blows.
Quiet ones, loud ones,
shy ones, proud ones…
It's FLOWER RESPECTFUL,
you know."

"Does purple love the sun like you do?"

"I guess… he smiles when he sees it."

"You can learn a lot from the SUN.
It shines on every flower.
Nice ones, mean ones, rolling ones, clean ones…
and even those who won't shower!"

"Do the bees visit purple like they visit you?"

"Yes Mom, but bees are colorblind."

"No son… bees are **COLOR RESPECTFUL**."

"*You can learn a lot from* **BEES.**
Bees visit every color.
They respect each flower for what's on the inside.
Each color's as good as all others."

12

"So if purple has roots…
and drinks the same water as you do…
and dances in the wind…
and smiles at the sun…
and gets buzzed by bees…

HE must be
a lot like YOU!"

"Well I still don't like him."

"Why not?"

"Because he's different. He's purple, and he shouldn't even be growing in this flower patch!"

"But how can you dislike someone you don't even know?"

"Huh?"

"Son, I think you are growing in the WRONG DIRECTION."

"When it comes to our petals,
there is no right or wrong.

Only different…
and different is

beautiful.

Like the notes you hear in a song."

"Somebody taught you to be judgmental.
You've learned how to feel this way.
But now is the time to open your heart.
Purple's different… and that's okay."

"You may feel unsure when you see a flower whose petals are not blue.

But the world would be very boring, if all flowers were just like you."

17

"There are differences in all of us…
on the inside and the out.

Learning how to be FLOWER RESPECTFUL
is what the world should be about."

"It's time to grow in a different direction,
and **knowledge** is the KEY!
Learn all you can about differences,
and then you will start to see."

"You can stop being judgmental,
if you can learn to celebrate
how every flower is unique.
And that makes a garden

GREAT!"

19

"You and purple need to learn
to grow alongside each other.
Recognize and respect the differences you have,
and get along with one another."

"But that's not the way it is now.
And that's not the way it used to be either."

"You're right."

"But all flowers need to start growing in the *right direction*."

"We ALL need to GROW UP"

21

"In order to grow in the right direction, you first must **OPEN YOUR HEART.** *If you can learn to celebrate differences, being judgmental won't pull you apart."*

Trust & Communication

"It's all about BUILDING RELATIONSHIPS, *based on* **communication** *and* trust. *Ask questions and be a good listener. Talking is a* **MUST!"**

"Trust is something that is earned.
It takes patience and some time.

If you and purple can talk and trust,
you'll get along just fine."

"*Just try it out with purple.
And if it works, tell the other blues.
Change is NEVER easy,
but I know it can start with* YOU!"

I thought about everything Mom told me,
and decided she might be right.

I DON'T
want to
GROW
IN THE
WRONG
DIRECTION.

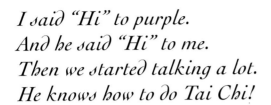

I said "Hi" to purple.
And he said "Hi" to me.
Then we started talking a lot.
He knows how to do Tai Chi!

We talked and listened.
 We learned how to trust.
We are a lot the same!
Purple taught me

SO MUCH STUFF!

And I let him play my new game.

We ended up becoming great friends.
I introduced him to the others.
Most of them are coming around.
Now purple's like one of our brothers.

My mom was right – a great flower patch
needs **different** styles, ideas, and colors.
If we can stop being so judgmental
We can get along better with others.

28

I feel like I'm growing
in the right direction now.
I know talking and
trusting is KEY.
Prejudice is learned and hurtful,
but ending it starts with

ME!

TALKING to Children
About Being JUDGMENTAL

By nature, children are not judgmental. They are not born to make damaging assumptions about others who seem different. In fact, children are gifted with an innate sense of justice and a deep level of respect for everyone.

Unfortunately, we teach our kids how to be judgmental.

Children who grow up in environments where differences are respected, acknowledged, and explained are much less likely to belittle or demean others for being different. To encourage understanding and greater acceptance of differences, here are some helpful strategies you can use in your home or classroom…

1. **Talk openly about differences.** Knowledge is KEY! Whether you draw attention to it or not, toddlers and children easily notice differences in people. Discussing these differences can make the unfamiliar less scary and threatening, and help reduce prejudice.

2. **Be a role model.** If you associate and connect with people who are different from you (ethnically, religiously, racially, politically, culturally, socio-economically, etc.), your children are more likely to be open and welcoming to others, too. Show respect to everyone, even those who may not share your beliefs, background, perspective, or lifestyle. Expose children to diversity-rich events, celebrate diverse classrooms, and cultivate friendships and relationships with people from all different walks of life.

"I don't like that man. I must get to know him better."
~ Abraham Lincoln

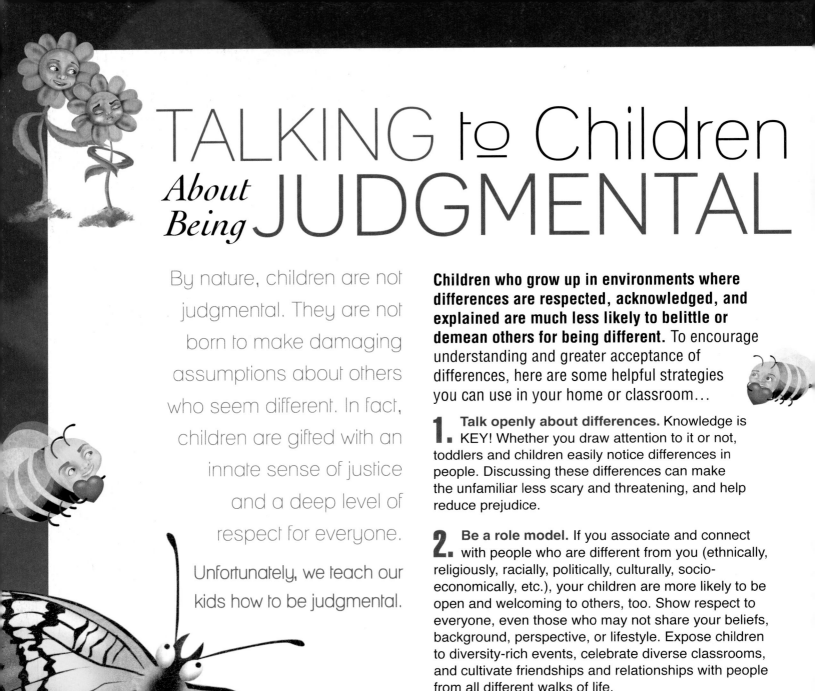

3. Look for teachable moments to highlight how people are just people.

CHILD: "Duncan is such a weirdo! He makes really strange grunts and flaps his arms all the time. I don't get it!"

PARENT/TEACHER: "Duncan has Autism. His brain is very unique, and it works differently than yours. When he moves his arms, he's expressing emotion. Duncan isn't weird, he's different. And different is okay."

4. Make your messages age-appropriate. When children are young, help them comprehend the often complicated issues of prejudice, diversity, and equality by using honest and respectful words they can understand. As they mature, supplement this healthy dialogue with real-world exposure to diverse people and environments.

5. Practice and model empathy and compassion. Capitalize on opportunities to teach empathy. Start by having children practice how to express their concerns using statements such as, "I know how sad you are about what just happened," and then have them follow their expressions of concern with offers of help. Also, teach and emphasize the **GOLDEN RULE: Treat others as you want them to treat you.**

6. Reward good behavior. When you see children interacting appropriately and joyfully with others who are different or showing genuine concern for the fair and equitable treatment of others, let them know you appreciate their kindness using verbal praise, a warm embrace or other gesture.

In order for children to truly celebrate and appreciate differences in people, they must be able to understand and make sense of those differences. Building effective human relationships with all types of people is a great way to gain this understanding.

Trust Communication

Always remember, in order for any human relationship to be successful, *trust* and **communication** must be present.

"It is time for parents to teach young people early on that in diversity there is beauty and there is strength."
~ Maya Angelou

Boys Town Press Books by Julia Cook

Building RELATIONSHIPS

Kid-friendly books to teach social skills

978-1-944882-05-1

TABLE TALK A book about table manners
978-1-934490-97-6

978-1-934490-30-3

978-1-934490-39-6

978-1-934490-47-1

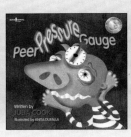
978-1-934490-48-8

978-1-934490-62-4

978-1-934490-86-0

Reinforce the social skills RJ learns in each book. *

BEST ME I Can Be

978-1-934490-43-3
978-1-934490-49-5
978-1-934490-67-9

Other Titles: The Worst Day of My Life Ever!, I Just Don't Like the Sound of NO!, Sorry, I Forgot to Ask!, and Teamwork Isn't My Thing, and I Don't Like to Share!
Accompanying posters sets and activity guides are available.

COMMUNICATE with **Confidence**

Help kids master the art of communicating.

978-1-934490-76-1
978-1-934490-58-7

Other Title: Well, I Can Top That!

978-1-944882-08-2

CHEATERS Never Prosper
Responsible ME!
But It's Not My Fault!
The PROCRASTINATOR
978-1-934490-8...
978-1-944882-09-9

Other Titles:
That Rule Doesn't Apply to Me! and Baditude!

BOYS TOWN® Press
BoysTownPress.org

For information on Boys Town, its Education Model®, Common Sense Parenting®, and training programs:
boystowntraining.org | boystown.org/parenting
training@BoysTown.org | 1-800-545-5771

For parenting and educational books and other resources:
BoysTownPress.org
btpress@BoysTown.org | 1-800-282-665